Loco Dog and the
Dust Devil
IN THE RAILYARD

BY MARCY HELLER
ILLUSTRATED BY NANCY POES

AZRO PRESS • SANTA FE • 2007

ISBN 978-1-929115-17-4
Library of Congress Control Number: 2007937836
Copyright © 2007 by Azro Press

Book designed by Marcy Heller

Printed in Canada by Friesens Book Division

Author's dedication:
To my daughter Bevin,
and to a longtime friend whose creativity
has sparked mine many times. Sally Blakemore,
part of this book belongs to you!

Artist's dedication:
To my beloved granddaughter, Elsa Maile Shilling.

Once upon a time, in the center of a dusty railyard, in a small southwestern town, there lived a large black dog. His name was Loco, short for Locomotive. He lived in the railroad office in the old railway depot. On cold snowy nights, he liked to curl up next to the black iron woodstove in the corner.

In the summer, he slept right outside the door. Loco always got up with the yardman when he walked the railyard. They made sure the tracks were clear.

L

oco was a favorite with the children in the town. He greeted them with lots of happy tail wagging whenever they came to the depot. He chased their balls and always brought them right back. He nudged them with his cold wet nose when he heard the sound of the locomotive starting up.

Loco followed them to the edge of the railyard right up to the sidewalk when they had to leave, and always sat down and wagged his tail as they called good-bye. But he never left his territory in the railyard, not even when the children tried to coax him with dog biscuits.

One wild, wet, and windy spring night, Loco was sleeping uneasily next to the desk in the railway office. Over the radio came a loud squawk, silence, and then the excited voice of the engineer heading into town on the 9:20 train.

He yelled, "It's the 9:20! I can't slow her down! My brakes have failed! Clear the tracks!"

The yardman ran outside. Loco was right on his heels. They saw bobbing headlights coming towards the tracks.

The yardman spotted Mr. Martinez in his old pickup truck rattling into the railyard to set up early for the farmers' market the next day. In the back of the pickup hunched Mr. Martinez's twelve-year-old grandson, Justin. Justin always helped his grandfather set up the trestle tables and unload the boxes.

The yardman waved his lantern at the truck frantically! But Mr. Martinez was looking the other way, at a big, black dust devil whirling down the tracks.

The yardman called out to Mr. Martinez, but the whistling locomotive shrieked even louder.

Mr. Martinez drove on, gazing at the dust devil zooming into the railyard. Loco galloped toward the truck. Justin looked up and saw the train approaching just as his grandfather began to bump slowly over the tracks. He hammered on the back window, but his grandfather was playing his old truck radio so loudly that he couldn't hear ANYTHING.

Justin stood up in the swaying pickup. The train was heading right for him. As the truck bumped up onto the tracks, he lost his balance and fell backwards out of the truck bed, towards the tracks.

A black streak charged up into the air and gave Justin a hard push, back into the pickup truck.

"WHOOOOOOOO!" wailed the locomotive.

As the train roared through the railyard, the dust devil soared over it and swallowed up the body of the dog. By the time the yardman got to the tracks, there was nothing to be seen of Loco.

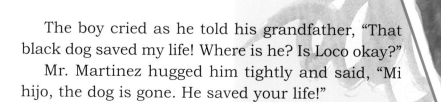

The boy cried as he told his grandfather, "That black dog saved my life! Where is he? Is Loco okay?"

Mr. Martinez hugged him tightly and said, "Mi hijo, the dog is gone. He saved your life!"

The yardman searched all around. "Loco, come here boy!" he called. He stayed out in the rain and wind for two hours and searched everywhere, but there was no Loco. There was not even a drop of blood on the tracks!

The engineer on the speeding train slowed the train to a stop by riding up the big hill outside of town. "Loco, where are you?" he called. Silence.

The yardman and the children of the town looked for Loco every day.

Finally, they sadly gave up. No big black dog to play catch with. No more happy greetings and fond farewells at the sidewalk.

Where could the dog have vanished to? No one had an answer. The weeks rolled by, but none of them forgot Loco and the special way he saved Justin's life.

Justin felt especially bad about Loco. Sometimes, late at night, he cried for the brave dog. In the daytime, he went to school, and kept helping his grandfather at the farmers' market on Saturdays.

His grandfather paid him a little bit of money every week. Justin was saving his money to go to an art school someday.

One Friday night as they were loading the pickup with boxes of greens, squash and tomatoes, his grandfather said, "Justin, why don't you buy yourself a big sketch pad and some paint and crayons?"

Justin said, "But Abuelo, I've been too sad to practice my drawing since Loco died."

Mr. Martinez said, "I know, Justin, but I have a feeling that this is the way out of your sadness for you."

Justin told his grandfather that he would get the art supplies, but he kept putting off the trip to the art store. The weeks and months rolled by, and Justin had almost forgotten his dream of becoming an artist.

The long, cold, snowy winter settled in, and the yardman looked sadly at the corner next to the woodstove where Loco used to sleep.

The spring finally blew in with its wild, windy days. It was just about a year ago that Justin almost died and Loco disappeared.

Justin decided that he would thank Loco by painting a picture of him. First he drew a small picture on a notebook-sized piece of paper. It was very good, but it was missing something.

Justin thought and thought and finally came up with the answer. The drawing was too small! What if he made it dog-sized? Justin taped lots of small pieces of paper together, but that didn't work.

"I know," nodded his grandfather, and he took the boy to the newspaper office. There, Justin got an end roll of newsprint. It was nice and wide and he could un-roll it as far as he needed.

H e got to work. He sketched a picture of Lobo running hard, stretched out in a lope like he used to be when he chased the children's balls. Then he mixed up a beautiful blue-black color, just like Loco's fur in the sunlight. He carefully painted the dog and finished up by painting in Loco's big brown eyes.

He taped the picture to the wall and stepped back to look at it. He jumped in surprise. The portrait of Loco looked EXACTLY like the real dog.

"Mom, come look at this!" he shouted to his mother. "I painted Loco!"

The next day, Justin took his painting down to the rail-yard to show the yardman. It was a cool, windy afternoon, exactly one year since the railyard accident that took Loco.

"Why, if that isn't Loco himself!" the yardman marveled at the art. "Thank you for showing it to me!"

Justin rolled the painting up and went out the door of the depot.
There was the spot where Loco used to sleep on warm nights.

Justin wandered over to the tracks. "Loco, we all loved you so
much! Why did you have to leave us?"

Justin sank down on the dusty ground and cried for a while. When he wiped his eyes, he looked at the sky and saw a black dust devil approaching. It was just like the one last year!

The dust devil swirled down the tracks. Justin froze. Dust flew everywhere and some of it stung Justin's eyes.

He dropped his drawing to rub his eyes and the wind caught it and whipped it up into the sky immediately. Justin cried out and reached out for his painting. The dust devil hovered over his head with the painting dancing just out of reach. Then it vanished overhead in a big black WHOOSH!

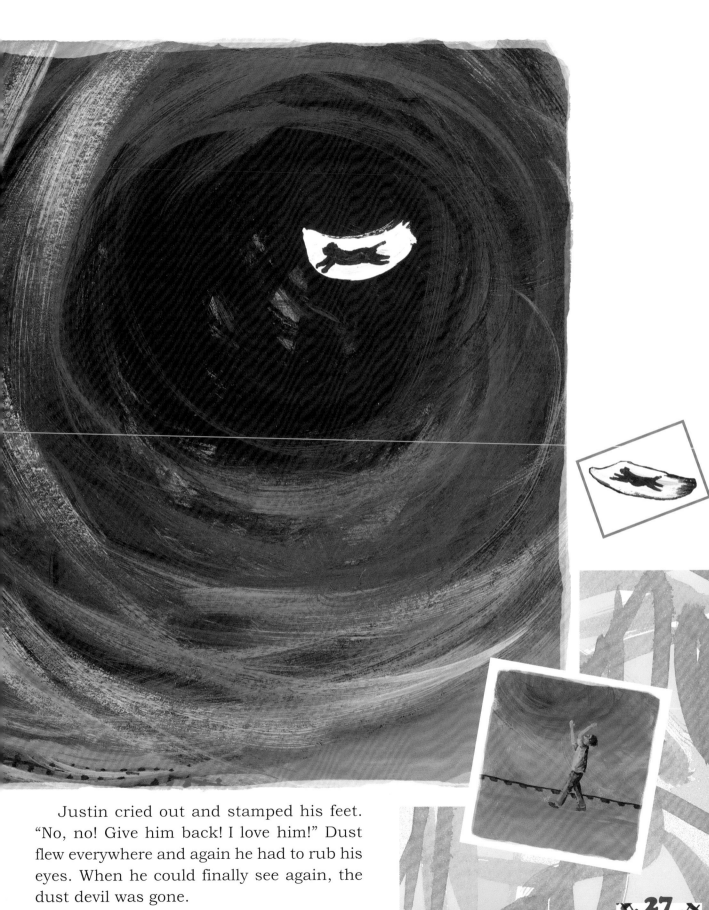

Justin cried out and stamped his feet.
"No, no! Give him back! I love him!" Dust
flew everywhere and again he had to rub his
eyes. When he could finally see again, the
dust devil was gone.

27

hat was that on the other side of the tracks? It looked like a big black dog!

"Loco, is that you?" Justin whispered. It was! There was the big black dog happily wagging his tail and barking. Justin dropped to his knees and hugged the dog over and over.

The yardman came running out of the depot because he heard the familiar barking. He could not believe his eyes.

"LOCO! You're back!" he shouted.

The happy reunions went on between the dog and the children for days. The adults of the town never understood how Loco had returned, but the children of the town knew.